The Polar Bear Paddle

David Bedford
Karen Sapp

QED Publishing

Alfie the polar bear **loved** water.

He could float quietly like a humpback whale.

He could tumble like a
blurry snowball.

And he could swim, too.
But he only ever swam in the baby pool.

Alfie could only do **the Polar Bear Paddle.**

"You're too big for the baby pool,"
said Alfie's older brothers.
"Why don't you swim in the sea with us?"
"Will you show me how?" said Alfie.

"No, we're too busy!" said Alfie's brothers,
and they swam away together.

Alfie watched Diving Bird diving in the sea.

Plop!

"Maybe Diving Bird will help me," Alfie thought.

SPLOSH!

Alfie was in the sea!

He tried wriggling and squiggling like Seal.

He flapped his arms like Diving Bird.

But in the end he did the Polar Bear Paddle.

When Alfie opened his eyes, he saw everyone clapping and waving!

"You were brilliant, Alfie!" shouted his brothers. "Will you show us how you dive in? Please, Alfie."
"Okay," said Alfie. "I will!"

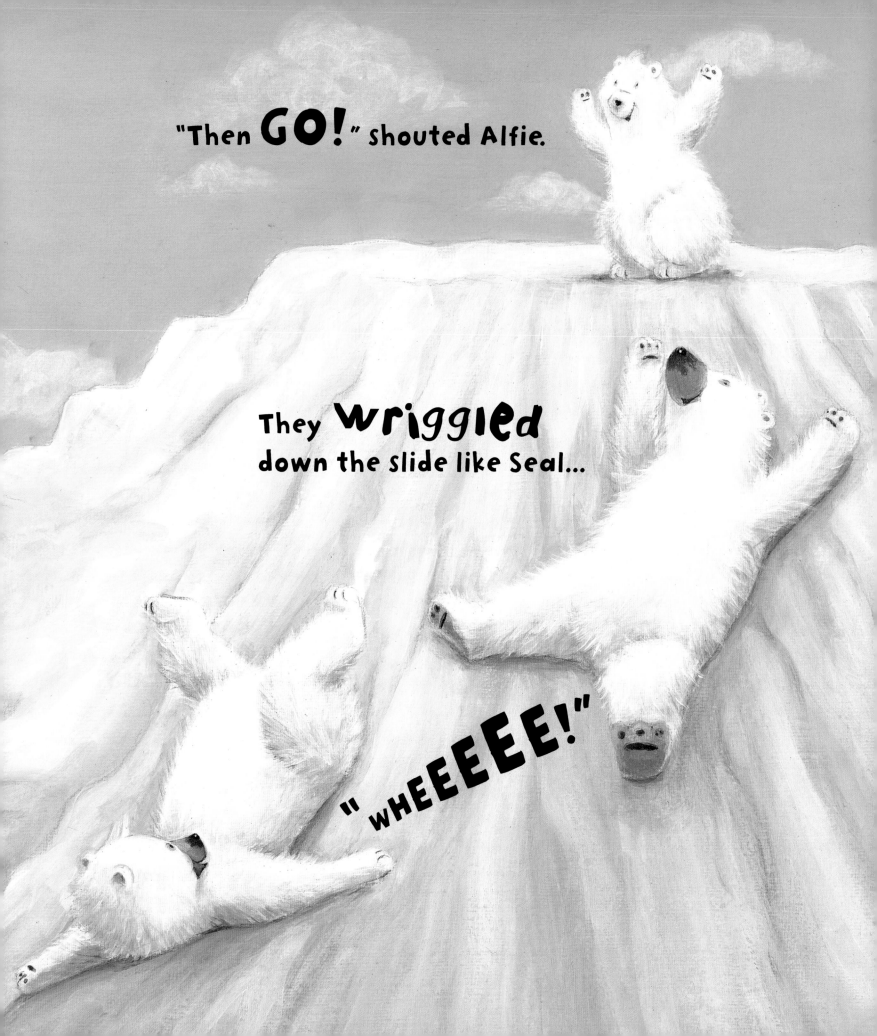

"Then **GO!**" shouted Alfie.

They **wriggled**
down the slide like Seal...

"**wHEEEEE!**"

They flapped through the air like Diving Bird...

After that, Alfie was happy to swim
in the sea like a polar bear.

"It's called the Polar Bear Paddle!"
Alfie told his brothers.
And he soon showed everyone how to do it!

Notes for parents and teachers

- Before you read this book to a child or children, look at the front cover and ask what they think the story is about. Then read the title.

- Read the story to the children and then ask them to read it to you, helping them with unfamiliar words and praising them for their efforts.

- Ask the children if they know where polar bears live. Discuss how the bears keep warm in very cold water, what they eat and where they have their homes.

- Do any of the children go swimming in a pool, or have they swum in the sea? Ask them to show you what they think the polar bear paddle would look like.

- Alfie was scared to go out of his baby pool. Do the children think he was brave to go swimming in the sea? Discuss with them what it means to be brave.

- Make a play of the story. One child can be Alfie, others his brothers and Diving Bird. Others can make the noises of the sea and the seal splashing through the water.

- Ask the children if they can remember who helped Alfie to swim in the sea.

- Next time the children go swimming, ask them to try doing the polar bear paddle with their arms. Talk about how this movement helps to pull them through the water.

- Ask the children to draw pictures of Alfie and the other characters in the story, using the illustrations in the book to help them. Use paints, crayons or coloured pencils to make them more colourful.

Copyright © QED Publishing 2009

First published in the UK in 2009 by
QED Publishing
A Quarto Group Company
226 City Road
London EC1V 2TT

www.qed-publishing.co.uk

ISBN 978 1 84835 239 1

Printed and bound in China

Author David Bedford
Illustrator Karen Sapp
Designer Alix Wood
Project Editor Heather Amery

Publisher Steve Evans
Creative Director Zeta Davies
Managing Editor Amanda Askew